Poetry for Youn

Edgar Allan Poe

Edited by Brod Bagert

Illustrations by Carolynn Cobleigh

STERLING

New York / London

www.sterlingpublishing.com/kids

A MAGNOLIA EDITIONS BOOK

STERLING and the distinctive Sterling logo are registered trademarks of
Sterling Publishing Co., Inc.

Library of Congress Cataloging-in-Publication Data
Poe, Edgar Allan, 1809–1849
Poetry for young people / Edgar Allan Poe ; edited by Brod Bagert :
illustrated by Carolynn Cobleigh.
p. cm.
"A Magnolia Editions Book" —T.p. verso.
Includes index.
Summary: A collection of thirteen poems and eight prose selections from larger works.
ISBN 0-8069-0820-3
1. Children's poetry, American [1. American poetry. 2. Short stories]
I. Bagert, Brod. II. Cobleigh, Carolynn, ill. III. Title. IV. Title: Edgar Allan Poe,
poetry for young people.
PS2605.B34 1995
811'. 3—dc20 94—30774

Photograph p. 4: Courtesy of the Edgar Allan Museum of the Poe Foundation

2 4 6 8 10 9 7 5 3 1

First paperback edition published 2008
by Sterling Publishing Co., Inc.
387 Park Avenue South, New York, NY 10016

Distributed in Canada by Sterling Publishing
c/o Canadian Manda Group, 165 Dufferin Street
Toronto, Ontario, Canada M6K 3H6
Distributed in the United Kingdom by GMC Distribution Services
Castle Place, 166 High Street, Lewes, East Sussex, England BN7 1XU
Distributed in Australia by Capricorn Link (Australia) Pty. Ltd.
P.O. Box 704, Windsor, NSW 2756, Australia

Printed in China

Sterling ISBN 978-1-4027-6423-3

Contents

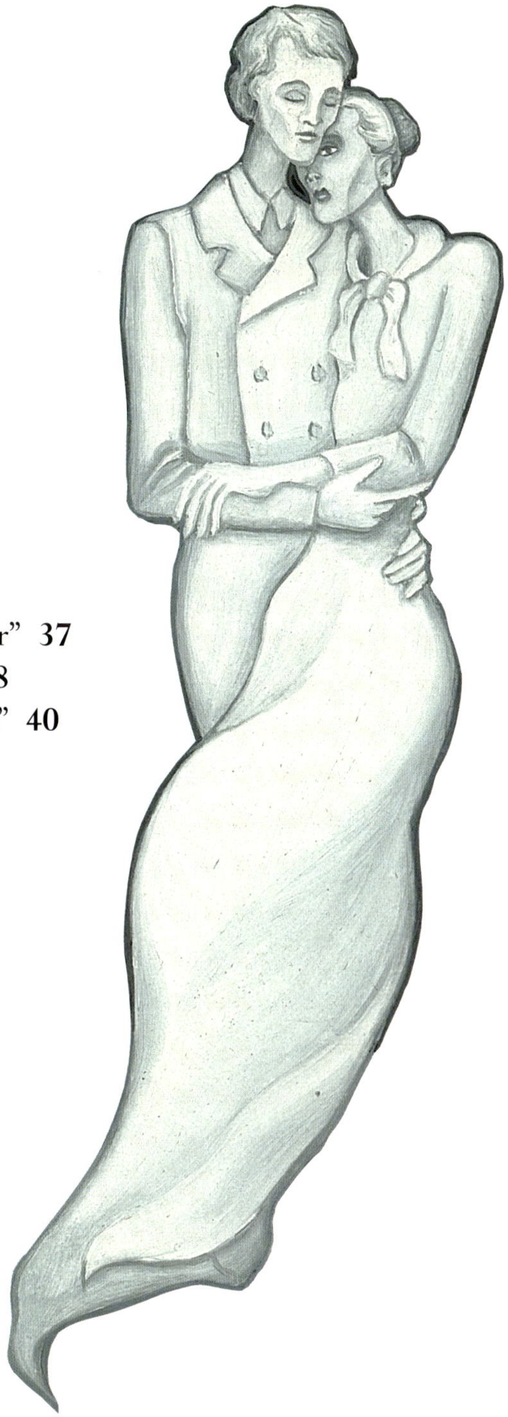

Introduction

MANY OF THE POEMS OF EDGAR ALLAN POE, "ANNABEL Lee" and "The Raven" in particular, are marked by deep sadness over the loss of a loved one. It is a sadness that began in Poe's childhood with his father's desertion and the death of his mother—a dark sadness that continued throughout his life.

In the early 1800s, Americans began to notice a beautiful young actress named Eliza Poe. She was married to David Poe, also an actor, and they had a son, William. Between 1806 and 1809, Eliza's and David's lives were changed by three important events. First, Eliza became a rising star in Boston. Theatergoers loved her beautiful and powerful presence onstage. Then, during the stormy winter of 1809, Eliza gave birth to a second son, Edgar. Finally, in that same year, the people at the Park Street Theater in New York, at the time America's largest and most famous theater, wooed the Poes to their stage. This was the break the Poes had been hoping for, so they moved to New York City.

New York audiences received Eliza with enthusiasm and affection, and it was apparent that she would soon be one of the most famous actresses in America. But her husband had little experience as an actor and, according to New York theater critics, even less talent. He missed performances because of "a sudden illness," which was really drunkenness. After only six weeks, David Poe deserted his wife and two sons and was never heard from again.

Eliza was left to care for her sons while she pursued her acting career. In December 1810, she gave birth to a girl, Rosalie. Although Eliza returned to the stage in the summer of 1811, she was very ill. She was bedridden by October and never performed again. Two months later, Eliza Poe said her last farewell to her children. Edgar was not yet three years old.

John and Frances Allan lived in Richmond, Virginia, and were avid theatergoers. Frances had helped care for Mrs. Poe and had become quite fond of little Edgar. The Allans had no children, so they decided to take Edgar in when his mother died, while William was sent to live with relatives in Baltimore and Rosalie was taken in by another Richmond family. Although he was never formally adopted, Poe lived with the Allans for a long time, and he honored them by taking Allan as his middle name.

John Allan was an independent, self-made merchant who believed in perseverance, hard work, and commitment to duty. He had a reputation for social benevolence, but was also a strict taskmaster. Frances was a dedicated homemaker, and she provided well for Poe. The Allans made sure that he received the benefits of an education, mostly at boarding schools. Allan said that by age six Poe was a "good scholar" and that he had learned to read Latin "pretty sharply." By age thirteen, Poe read the Latin poets with fluency, and he began to write poetry of his own. He also excelled in athletics: he was a good boxer, a fast runner, and an exceptional swimmer. He once swam six miles in the James River, and he set a school broad-jump record of 21 feet 6 inches.

Although Poe seemed happy, deep inside he was confused. Because he was never formally adopted, he felt uncertain about his position in the Allan family, and his doubt often made him cross and dejected. Allan interpreted Poe's behavior as a lack of gratitude. When Poe was sixteen and entering the University of Virginia, resentments between Poe and Allan were simmering beneath the surface.

While in college, Poe wrote his first story. Although most of Poe's stories are rather gloomy, this one was bright and funny. When he read the story to his friends, however, they teased him about it, so he threw it into the fire. Eventually, Poe learned to accept criticism—but it was too late to save his first story.

Poe was an excellent student, but he accumulated large debts. He claimed that Allan did not give him enough money and asked for more. Allan blamed Poe's lack of money on his drinking, gambling, and expensive tastes. At the end of his first year in college, Poe was several thousand dollars in debt, which Allan refused to pay. As a result, Poe could not return to college.

Poe returned to his birthplace and got a job, using his spare time to write poetry. There he published his first book, *Tamerlane and Other Poems*, but did not use his name, saying instead that it was written by "a Bostonian." By the time the book appeared, he had enlisted in the army. He was eighteen and a minor, so he should have obtained John Allan's consent to join. However, he did not want to tell Allan of his plans, so he enlisted under the name Edgar A. Perry and said he was twenty-two.

Poe did well in the army. A lieutenant said that he performed his duties "promptly and faithfully" and that he was "entirely free from drinking." On New Year's Day, 1829, Poe was made a sergeant major, the highest rank for a noncommissioned officer. But Poe was unhappy, so he told the truth about his age and requested an early discharge. The lieutenant agreed only if Poe would reconcile with John Allan. Poe sent Allan three letters, but Allan ignored them until eventually, softened by the death of his wife, he agreed to the reconciliation.

Poe had planned to be discharged so that he could attend the U.S. Military Academy at West Point. It took him a year to gain admission, and during that time he continued to write poetry. In November 1829, he published *Al Aaraaf*, using his real name. Although the book received mixed reviews, it did not go unnoticed.

About this time Poe and Allan began to quarrel again. Allan continued to provide less money than Poe thought he needed. Allan remarried, which made Poe feel rejected. Poe decided to leave West Point, but Allan refused to sign the required resignation papers, so Poe vowed that he would get himself dishonorably discharged, which he did in January 1831. After that, Poe and Allan had little contact, and when Allan died in 1834, there was no mention of Poe in his will.

After leaving West Point, Poe lived in New York for two years. There he published a new book that received little notice, much of it unfavorable. Hungry and disappointed, he went to Baltimore to live with his widowed aunt, Maria Poe Clemm, who was already caring for Poe's brother, William, an alcoholic. William died a few months later, leaving Poe alone with Maria and her daughter, Virginia.

In 1834 Poe got a job in Baltimore with a magazine, first as a contributor (in a single year he contributed eighty-three reviews, four essays, six poems, and three stories) and eventually as an editor. Poe made the magazine one of the nation's most respected publications. But three years later, he was fired because his alcoholism interfered with his job. It was obvious that Poe could no longer control his drinking. While sober, Poe wrote the words that made him famous, but he could not stop drinking completely. Poe once wrote to a friend, "During these long fits of absolute unconsciousness I drank—God only knows how often or how much."

Poe's frustration with his addiction is reflected in his story "The Cask of Amontillado," in which a victim is lured by his murderer's promise of a drink of wine into dark underground passages. The murderer places the victim in chains and begins to seal him behind a brick wall. As he places the last brick, the victim screams out for the wine he was promised. As in the story, Poe's addiction led him into dark places.

In 1837, Poe, age twenty-seven, married his first cousin Virginia, age thirteen, perhaps to secure his place in the Clemm household. Two years later, Poe's first collection of short stories, *Tales of the Grotesque and Arabesque,* was published. While some thought it was particularly gloomy, the book was generally received as the most powerful collection of short fiction ever published in America. Unfortunately, it was published during a recession, so only seven hundred fifty copies were printed, and those took three years to sell. Although Poe was becoming more famous, he was still poor, and both he and his wife were ill.

Poe's skill as a storyteller continued to grow. In 1841, he penned a detective story called "The Murders in the Rue Morgue." Although detective stories are common today, Poe wrote the first one, inventing a new literary form. In 1845, *The Raven and Other Poems* was published, a collection that includes "The Raven," one of the most popular poems ever written.

The Poes were married for ten years until, after a long illness, Virginia passed away. After she died, Poe collapsed and was nursed back to health by Marie Louise Shew, who inspired "The Beloved Physician," the lost poem of which a part appears in this book.

Poe once wrote that "the death of a beautiful woman is, unquestionably, the most poetical topic in the world." It is a topic that Poe knew all too well: in his short lifetime, he had lost his mother, his foster mother, and his wife. There is little wonder why so many of his poems are about the death of a loved one.

In the years that followed, Poe pursued a number of women. In each instance, either his reputation or his drinking kept the women from marrying him. At one point, he even returned to Richmond and became reacquainted with his old girlfriend, Elmira Royster, who was now wealthy and recently widowed. On September 27, 1849, he left Richmond for Baltimore, the first stop on a business trip. No one knows what went on during the next week of Poe's life. On October 3, a printer named Joseph Walker noticed Poe, whom he described as "rather worse for wear," in a Baltimore tavern. Walker immediately notified a friend of Poe's, Joseph Snodgrass, who promptly had Poe admitted to a hospital.

For days Poe slipped in and out of consciousness. Just when he seemed to be improving, his condition would take a turn for the worse. He became delirious, ranting and raving for several hours. At three o'clock on the morning of Sunday, October 7, 1849, Poe said, "Lord help my poor soul!" and died. He was only forty years old.

Edgar Allan Poe was a master storyteller and a great poet. Three of his poems, "Annabel Lee," "The Raven," and "The Bells," are among the most beautiful and moving poems in the English language. All three were written in the last five years of his life. Like his mother, Poe was brilliantly talented. Like his father, Poe was destroyed by alcoholism. Sadly, Poe died when he was just beginning to achieve his full power as a great poet.

A Note to Parents

What we have done in this volume is a little unusual, and we'd like to explain why and how we did it. You will not find the last eight "poems" in this book in any of Poe's other collections. This is because Poe did not actually write them as poems; they were originally part of larger prose works.

Beautiful poetic passages can often be found in longer prose works. These powerful moments gleam like diamonds in the silver setting of the surrounding prose. Such gems are often the poetic equal of the author's "official" poems. This seems especially true of nineteenth-century American writers, and Poe is no exception. So we searched his stories to find passages which, although published as prose, stand out as poetry. The idea is to give the full range of Poe's poetic voice, so children can feel the full power of his poetry.

When we found one of these passages, we faced the task of presenting it in poetic form. This required us to "tinker" with the work of a great writer, so we were as delicate as possible. While some words and phrases were omitted and the text was rearranged into verses, what remains is entirely the work of Edgar Allan Poe. But still we wondered: "Would Mr. Poe have approved?"

We decided he would. Poe believed a poem was a communication between the poet and the reader, and he put the needs of the reader first. In his essay "The Poetic Principle," he wrote, "A poem deserves its title only inasmuch as it excites, by elevating the soul." Since Poe defined poetry in terms of its ability to excite the soul of the reader, we think he would probably approve of our approach. We suspect that he might even feel gratified to know that, in this way, the children of our generation can hear the full beauty of his poetic voice and come to love his poetry.

ALONE

When we read this poem we learn that since his childhood Poe had believed he was different from other people. This belief made him feel lonely, and his loneliness was like a "demon" that he saw everywhere he turned.

From childhood's hour I have not been
As others were—I have not seen
As others saw—I could not bring
My passions from a common spring—
From the same source I have not taken
My sorrow—I could not awaken
My heart to joy at the same tone—
And all I ever lov'd—I lov'd alone—
Then—in my childhood—in the dawn
Of a most stormy life—was drawn
From every depth of good and ill
The mystery which binds me still—
From the torrent, or the fountain—
From the red cliff of the mountain—
From the sun that 'round me roll'd
In its autumn tint of gold—
From the lightning in the sky
As it pass'd me flying by—
From the thunder, and the storm—
And the cloud that took the form
(When the rest of Heaven was blue)
Of a demon in my view—

torrent–*flood of water*

Annabel Lee

In this poem a man tells of his love for a girl named Annabel Lee. The poem is happy at first, but turns sad when we learn that Annabel Lee has died. Then we realize that the man has gone mad when he accuses the angels of killing Annabel Lee out of jealousy. This is a great poem to read out loud, for in it Poe has made the English language sound very musical.

It was many and many a year ago,
In a kingdom by the sea,
That a maiden there lived whom you may know
By the name of Annabel Lee;
And this maiden she lived with no other thought
Than to love and be loved by me.

I was a child and *she* was a child,
In this kingdom by the sea:
But we loved with a love that was more than love—
I and my Annabel Lee;
With a love that the winged seraphs of heaven
Coveted her and me.

---

seraphs–*angels* coveted–*wanted to take from*

And this was the reason that, long ago,
   In this kingdom by the sea.
A wind blew out of a cloud, chilling
   My beautiful Annabel Lee;
So that her high-born kinsmen came
   And bore her away from me,
To shut her up in a sepulchre
   In this kingdom by the sea.

The angels, not half so happy in heaven,
   Went envying her and me—
Yes!—that was the reason (as all men know,
   In this kingdom by the sea)
That the wind came out of the cloud by night,
   Chilling and killing my Annabel Lee.

But our love it was stronger by far than the love
   Of those who were older than we—
   Of many far wiser than we—
And neither the angels in heaven above,
   Nor the demons down under the sea,
Can ever dissever my soul from the soul
   Of the beautiful Annabel Lee,

For the moon never beams without bringing me dreams
   Of the beautiful Annabel Lee;
And the stars never rise but I feel the bright eyes
Of the beautiful Annabel Lee;
And so, all the night-tide, I lie down by the side
Of my darling—my darling—my life and my bride,
      In the sepulchre there by the sea,
      In her tomb by the sounding sea.

---

sepulchre–*tomb* dissever–*separate*

THE LAKE

The "lake" described in this poem is the Lake of the Dismal Swamp, which Poe visited as a young man. Legend holds that the lake is haunted by the ghosts of two lovers. A young man, unable to accept the death of the girl he loved, imagined that she was alive somewhere in the swamp, followed her there, and was never seen again.

In this poem, Poe describes how he felt when visiting the lake—how he found it beautiful by day but scary at night. Yet even as a child, Poe was delighted by the "terror."

In youth's spring, it was my lot
To haunt of the wide earth a spot
The which I could not love the less;
So lovely was the loneliness
Of a wild lake, with black rock bound,
And the tall pines that tower'd around.

But when the night had thrown her pall
Upon that spot—as upon all,
And the wind would pass me by
In its still melody,
My infant spirit would awake
To the terror of that lone lake.

Yet that terror was not fright—
But a tremulous delight,
And a feeling undefin'd
Springing from a darken'd mind.

Death was in that poison'd wave
And in its gulf a fitting grave
For him who thence could solace bring
To his dark imagining;
Whose wild'ring thought could even make
An Eden of that dim lake.

---

pall–*cloth covering a coffin* tremulous–*affected with trembling* solace–*comfort* wild'ring–*bewildering*

The Raven

This is probably Poe's most famous poem. "The Raven" is a great poem to read out loud. It's a bit long, but with some practice you can read it with the kind of expression that will give your friends goosebumps.

The poem opens on a man alone in his house. He is very sad over the death of Lenore, the woman he loved, and he is reading to relieve his sorrow. He hears what he thinks is a person knocking at his door. Eventually he learns that it is not a person at all but a bird—a raven. At first he is amused, but soon grows sad. The bird can say only one word, "Nevermore," and that word reminds him that nothing can bring back his lost Lenore.

Once upon a midnight dreary, while I pondered, weak and weary,
Over many a quaint and curious volume of forgotten lore—
While I nodded, nearly napping, suddenly there came a tapping,
As of some one gently rapping, rapping at my chamber door.
"'Tis some visitor," I muttered, "tapping at my chamber door—
Only this and nothing more."

Ah, distinctly I remember it was in the bleak December;
And each separate dying ember wrought its ghost upon the floor.
Eagerly I wished the morrow;—vainly I had sought to borrow
From my books surcease of sorrow—sorrow for the lost Lenore—
For the rare and radiant maiden whom the angels name Lenore—
Nameless here for evermore.

And the silken, sad, uncertain rustling of each purple curtain
Thrilled me—filled me with fantastic terrors never felt before;
So that now, to still the beating of my heart, I stood repeating
"'Tis some visitor entreating entrance at my chamber door—
Some late visitor entreating entrance at my chamber door;—
This it is and nothing more."

Presently my soul grew stronger; hesitating then no longer,
"Sir," said I, "or Madam, truly your forgiveness I implore;
But the fact is I was napping, and so gently you came rapping,
And so faintly you came tapping, tapping at my chamber door,
That I scarce was sure I heard you"—here I opened wide the door;—
Darkness there and nothing more.

---

lore–*legend* surcease–*an end* entreating–*requesting*

Deep into that darkness peering, long I stood there wondering, fearing,
Doubting, dreaming dreams no mortal ever dared to dream to dream before;
But the silence was unbroken, and the darkness gave no token,
And the only word there spoken was the whispered word, "Lenore?"
This I whispered, and an echo murmured back the word, "Lenore!"
Merely this and nothing more.

Back into the chamber turning, all my soul within me burning,
Soon again I heard a tapping somewhat louder than before.
"Surely," said I, "surely that is something at my window lattice;
Let me see, then, what thereat is, and this mystery explore—
Let my heart be still a moment and this mystery explore;—
'Tis the wind and nothing more!"

Open here I flung the shutter, when, with many a flirt and flutter,
In there stepped a stately Raven of the saintly days of yore;
Not the least obeisance made he; not a minute stopped or stayed he;
But, with mien of lord or lady, perched above my chamber door—
Perched upon a bust of Pallas just above my chamber door—
Perched, and sat, and nothing more.

Then this ebony bird beguiling my sad fancy into smiling,
By the grave and stern decorum of the countenance it wore,
"Though thy crest be shorn and shaven, thou," I said, "art sure no craven,
Ghastly grim and ancient Raven wandering from the Nightly shore —
Tell me what thy lordly name is on the Night's Plutonian shore!"
Quoth the Raven "Nevermore."

Much I marvelled this ungainly fowl to hear discourse so plainly,
Though its answer little meaning—little relevancy bore;
For we cannot help agreeing that no living human being
Ever yet was blessed with seeing bird above his chamber door—
Bird or beast upon the sculptured bust above his chamber door,
With such name as "Nevermore."

---

token–*clue* lattice–*window covering made from strips of wood* yore–*long ago*
obeisance–*sign of obediance* mien–*appearance* Pallas–*Athena, goddess of wisdom*
ebony–*black* beguiling–*charming* decorum–*dignity* countenance–*facial expression* craven–*coward*
Plutonian–*deathly* ungainly–*clumsy* discourse–*speech* relevancy–*importance*

But the Raven, sitting lonely on the placid bust, spoke only
That one word, as if his soul in that one word he did outpour.
Nothing further then he uttered—not a feather then he fluttered—
Till I scarcely more than muttered "Other friends have flown before—
On the morrow will *he* leave me, as my Hopes have flown before."
  Then the bird said "Nevermore."

Startled at the stillness broken by reply so aptly spoken,
"Doubtless," said I, "what it utters is its only stock and store
Caught from some unhappy master whom unmerciful Disaster
Followed fast and followed faster till his songs one burden bore—
Till the dirges of his Hope that melancholy burden bore
  Of 'Never—nevermore.'"

But the Raven still beguiling all my sad fancy into smiling,
Straight I wheeled a cushioned seat in front of bird and bust and door;
Then, upon the velvet sinking, I betook myself to linking
Fancy unto fancy, thinking what this ominous bird of yore—
What this grim, ungainly, gaunt, and ominous bird of yore
  Meant in croaking "Nevermore."

This I sat engaged in guessing, but no syllable expressing
To the fowl whose fiery eyes now burned into my bosom's core;
This and more I sat divining, with my head at ease reclining
On the cushion's velvet lining that the lamp-light gloated o'er,
But whose velvet-violet lining with the lamp-light gloating o'er,
  She shall press, ah, nevermore!

Then, methought the air grew denser, perfumed from an unseen censer
Swung by seraphim whose foot-falls tinkled on the tufted floor.
"Wretch," I cried, "thy God hath lent thee—by these angels he has sent thee
Respite—respite and nepenthe from the memories of Lenore;
Quaff, oh quaff this kind nepenthe and forget this lost Lenore!"
  Quoth the Raven "Nevermore."

dirges–*burial songs* ominous–*spooky* divining–*coming to a conclusion* denser–*thicker*
censer–*incense burner* seraphim–*angel* nepenthe–*drink that causes forgetfulness* quaff–*to drink*

"Prophet!" said I, "thing of evil!—prophet still, if bird or devil!—
Whether Tempter sent, or whether tempest tossed thee here ashore,
Desolate yet all undaunted, on this desert land enchanted—
On this home by Horror haunted—tell me truly, I implore—
Is there—*is* there balm in Gilead?—tell me—tell me, I implore!"
Quoth the Raven "Nevermore."

"Prophet!" said I, "thing of evil!—prophet still, if bird or devil!
By that Heaven that bends above us—by that God we both adore—
Tell this soul with sorrow laden if, within the distant Aidenn,
It shall clasp a sainted maiden whom the angels name Lenore—
Clasp a rare and radiant maiden whom the angels name Lenore."
Quoth the Raven "Nevermore."

"Be that word our sign of parting, bird or fiend!" I shrieked, upstarting—
"Get thee back into the tempest and the Night's Plutonian shore!
Leave no black plume as a token of that lie thy soul hath spoken!
Leave my loneliness unbroken!—quit the bust above my door!
Take thy beak from out my heart, and take thy form from off my door!"
Quoth the Raven "Nevermore."

And the Raven, never flitting, still is sitting, *still* is sitting
On the pallid bust of Pallas just above my chamber door;
And his eyes have all the seeming of a demon's that is dreaming,
And the lamp-light o'er him streaming throws his shadow on the floor;
And my soul from out that shadow that lies floating on the floor
Shall be lifted—nevermore!

tempter–*devil* tempest–*storm* desolate–*alone* undaunted–*unafraid* balm–*soothing oil*
Gilead–*ancient place in the Middle East known for its balm* Aidenn–*Aidin, a rich province of Turkey*
plume–*feather* pallid–*pale*

To Helen

This is a romantic poem in the voice of a man who is standing outside the house of a woman named Helen. It is nighttime. Helen, holding an oil lamp, steps in front of the window. We suspect that she is signaling to someone. The man outside, very happy to see her, tells us that Helen's beauty is like a ship sent to bring him home from the sea.

Helen, thy beauty is to me
Like those Nicaean barks of yore,
That gently, o'er a perfumed sea,
The weary, way-worn wanderer bore
To his own native shore.

On desperate seas long wont to roam,
Thy hyacinth hair, thy classic face,
Thy Naiad airs have brought me home
To the glory that was Greece,
And the grandeur that was Rome.

Lo! in yon brilliant window-niche
How statue-like I see thee stand,
The agate lamp within thy hand!
Ah, Psyche, from the regions which
Are Holy-Land!

Nicaean–*from the ancient Byzantine city of Nicaea, now the Turkish city of Iznik*
wont–*used to or accustomed to* hyacinth–*deep red* naiad–*river spirit* Psyche–*in Greek mythology, the beautiful wife of the god Cupid*

A Dream Within a Dream

In poetry, there are a few ideas we hear over and over again. It is as though certain thoughts live in the soul of every poet. This poem contains one of those ideas. In the second stanza, Poe tells us that the days of life slip through his fingers like grains of sand, and no matter how he tries, he cannot stop the passage of time. It is an idea that was repeated a hundred years later by another American, a man named Thornton Wilder, who wrote,"Do any human beings ever realize life while they live it? Every minute? No, the Saints and Poets, maybe they do some."

Take this kiss upon the brow!
And, in parting from you now,
This much let me avow—
You are not wrong, who deem
That my days have been a dream;
Yet if Hope has flown away
In a night, or in a day,
In a vision, or in none,
Is it therefore the less gone?
All that we see or seem
Is but a dream within a dream.

I stand amid the roar
Of a surf-tormented shore,
And I hold within my hand
Grains of the golden sand—
How few! yet how they creep
Through my fingers to the deep,
While I weep—while I weep!
O God! can I not grasp
Them with a tighter clasp?
O God! can I not save
One from the pitiless wave?
Is *all* that we see or seem
But a dream within a dream?

The Beloved Physician

This is a small part of a poem that was originally nine stanzas long. These few lines are all that remain. We find them quoted in a letter written by Marie Louise Shew, the lady to whom the poem was written. It was she who eventually lost or perhaps destroyed the poem.

In her letter she says, "I came up a country doctor's only daughter, with a taste for painting and a heart for loving all the world. I saved Mr. Poe's life at this time...at best, when he was well Mr. Poe's pulse beat only ten regular beats, after which it suspended or intermitted." Ms. Shew took care of Poe and nursed him back to health, and we suspect that she is the "beloved physician" referred to in the title of the poem.

In this poem, Poe describes how his heart beats ten times and then skips a beat. Without the rest of the poem, it is hard to hear exactly what he is trying to say. Yet we are lucky to have these few beautiful lines. They whisper a sense of calm—rest at last for a troubled soul.

The pulse beats ten and intermits.
God nerve the soul that ne'er forgets
In calm or storm, by night or day,
Its steady toil, its loyalty.

***

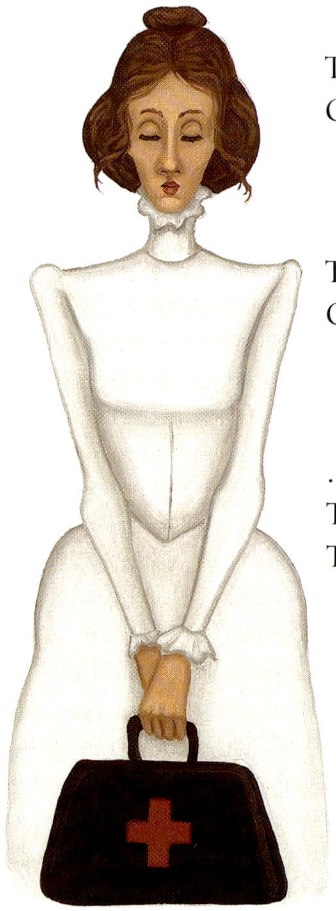

The pulse beats ten and intermits.
God shield the soul that ne'er forgets.

***

The pulse beats ten and intermits.
God guide the soul that ne'er forgets.

***

… so tired, so weary,
The soft head bows, the sweet eyes close;
The faithful heart yields to repose.

intermits–*stops for a moment* repose–*rest*

The Bells

Two years before his death, Poe met the Reverend Cotesworth P. Bronson. Reverend Bronson was an elocutionist, someone who reads poetry out loud with a lot of expression. He encouraged Poe to write poems that could be performed aloud for an audience. Poe agreed to try, and "The Bells" was one of the poems that grew out of the reverend's suggestion. Be sure to read this poem out loud so you can hear how the sound and the meaning of the poem work together.

"The Bells" occurs in four parts, and each part has a different set of bells. In the first part we hear the tinkle of silver sleigh bells, and we think of the joy of childhood. When we hear the wedding bells of the second part, we think of love and hope. The bells of the third part are brazen alarm bells whose shriek is a warning of fire in the night. These bells make us think of the tragedies life can hold as we grow older. In the final part we hear iron bells. "Every sound that floats from the rust within their throats is a groan." What kind of bells do you think these are?

1

Hear the sledges with the bells—
Silver bells!
What a world of merriment their melody foretells!
How they tinkle, tinkle, tinkle,
In the icy air of night!
While the stars that oversprinkle
All the Heavens, seem to twinkle
With a crystalline delight;
Keeping time, time, time,
In a sort of Runic rhyme,
To the tintinnabulation that so musically wells
From the bells, bells, bells, bells,
Bells, bells, bells—
From the jingling and the tinkling of the bells.

sledges–*sleighs* crystalline–*clear crystal* runic–*ancient* tintinnabulation–*sound of a bell ringing*

2

Hear the mellow wedding bells—
Golden bells!
What a world of happiness their harmony foretells!
Through the balmy air of night
How they ring out their delight!—
From the molten-golden notes
And all in tune
What a liquid ditty floats
To the turtle-dove that listens while she gloats
On the moon!
Oh, from out the sounding cells
What a gush of euphony voluminously wells! How it swells!
How it swells!
How it dwells
On the future!—how it tells
Of the rapture that impels
To the swinging and the ringing
Of the bells, bells, bells!—
Of the bells, bells, bells, bells,
Bells, bells, bells—
To the rhyming and the chiming of the bells!

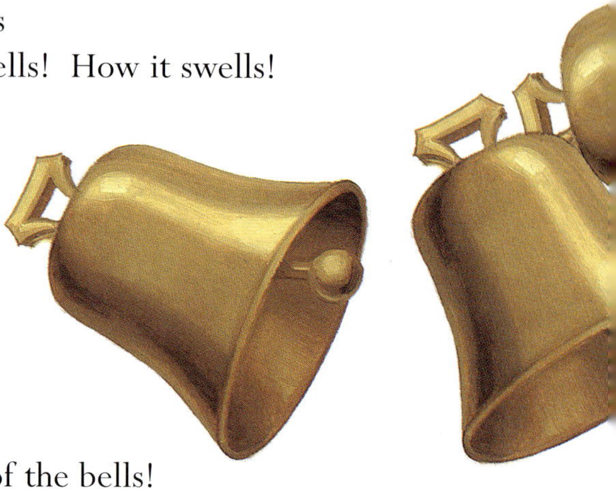

3

Hear the loud alarum bells—
Brazen bells!
What tale of terror, now, their turbulency tells!
In the startled ear of Night
How they scream out their affright!
Too much horrified to speak,
They can only shriek, shriek,
Out of tune,
In a clamorous appealing to the mercy of the fire—
In a mad expostulation with the deaf and frantic fire,
Leaping higher, higher, higher,

---

euphony–*pleasant sound* voluminously–*largely* rapture–*delightful feeling* impels–*pushes onward* alarum–*alarm* brazen–*rudely bold* turbulency–*violent movement* affright–*fear* expostulation–*attempt at persuading*

With a desperate desire
And a resolute endeavor
Now—now to sit, or never,
By the side of the pale-faced moon.
Oh, the bells, bells, bells!
What a tale their terror tells
Of despair!
How they clang and clash and roar!
What a horror they outpour
In the bosom of the palpitating air!
Yet the ear, it fully knows,
By the twanging
And the clanging,
How the danger ebbs and flows:—
Yes, the ear distinctly tells,
In the jangling
And the wrangling,
How the danger sinks and swells,
By the sinking or the swelling in the anger of the bells—
Of the bells—
Of the bells, bells, bells, bells,
Bells, bells, bells—
In the clamor and the clangor of the bells.

4

Hear the tolling of the bells—
Iron bells!
What a world of solemn thought their monody compels!
In the silence of the night
How we shiver with affright
At the melancholy meaning of the tone!
For every sound that floats
From the rust within their throats
Is a groan.
And the people—ah, the people

resolute–*determined* endeavor–*determined effort* palpitating–*throbbing*
monody–*death song* melancholy–*monotone*

They that dwell up in the steeple
All alone,
And who, tolling, tolling, tolling,
In that muffled monotone,
Feel a glory in so rolling
On the human heart a stone—
They are neither man nor woman—
They are neither brute nor human,
They are Ghouls:—
And their king it is who tolls:—
And he rolls, rolls, rolls, rolls
A Paean from the bells!
And his merry bosom swells
With the Paean of the bells!
And he dances and he yells;
Keeping time, time, time,
In a sort of Runic rhyme,
To the Paean of the bells—
Of the bells:—
Keeping time, time, time,
In a sort of Runic rhyme,
To the throbbing of the bells—
Of the bells, bells, bells—
To the sobbing of the bells:—
Keeping time, time, time,
As he knells, knells, knells,
In a happy Runic rhyme,
To the rolling of the bells—
Of the bells, bells, bells—
To the tolling of the bells—
Of the bells, bells, bells, bells,
Bells, bells, bells—
To the moaning and the groaning of the bells.

---

monotone–*single note*   ghouls–*evil graveyard spirits*   paean–*song of triumph*   knells–*rings*

Eldorado

In this poem a knight goes in search of Eldorado, the mythical city of gold. He never finds it, and as he is about to die, he asks another wandering spirit where the city can be found. The last stanza is the spirit's reply. There may be times, as you grow older, when these lines will ring true in your ears.

Gaily bedight,
A gallant knight,
In sunshine and in shadow,
Had journeyed long
Singing a song,
In search of Eldorado.

But he grew old—
This knight so bold—
And o'er his heart a shadow
Fell as he found
No spot of ground
That looked like Eldorado.

And, as his strength
Failed him at length,
He met a pilgrim shadow—
"Shadow," said he,
"Where can it be—
This land of Eldorado?"

"Over the Mountains
Of the Moon,
Down the Valley of the Shadow,
Ride, boldly ride."
The shade replied,—
"If you seek for Eldorado!"

---

bedight–*well-equipped*

Romance

This poem was one of Poe's favorites. He used it once as a preface and again as an introduction to books of his poems. He particularly liked the first five lines of the second stanza. Be careful: "romance" as used here does not mean "love"; it means an extravagant story based on things that cannot be true.

In the first stanza, Poe tells us that, as a child, his life was like a beautiful parakeet ("paroquet"), full of colorful stories that encouraged him to read and become wise beyond his years. In the second stanza, he tells us that his life as a young man was like a condor, a bird of prey that has no time for beauty. Then Poe predicts that there will come a more peaceful time in his life, and promises us that when that time comes, his heart will sing again like strings of a musical instrument.

1

Romance who loves to nod and sing
With drowsy head and folded wing
Among the green leaves as they shake
Far down within some shadowy lake
To me a painted paroquet
Hath been—a most familiar bird—
Taught me my alphabet to say—
To lisp my very earliest word
While in the wild wood I did lie
A child—with a most knowing eye.

2

Of late, eternal Condor years
So shake the very air on high
With tumult, as they thunder by,
I hardly have had time for cares
Thro' gazing on th' unquiet sky!
And, when an hour with calmer wings
Its down upon my spirit flings—
That little time with lyre and rhyme
To while away—forbidden things!
My heart would feel to be a crime
Did it not tremble with the strings!

condor–*large vulture* tumult–*disturbance* lyre–*small harp*

For Annie

This poem was written to Nancy Richmond, whose nickname was Annie. She was Poe's friend but not his "girlfriend." In a letter to her, Poe wrote, "I am so ill...in body and mind, that I feel I cannot live, unless I can feel your sweet, gentle, loving hand pressed upon my forehead—oh my pure, virtuous, generous, beautiful, beautiful sister Annie!"

This tender poem is about the healing power of her friendship. Poe is lying in bed. He has just overcome a "lingering illness" and he lies so still that you might think he is dead. But he is not dead; he is aglow "with the light of the love of my Annie." In this poem you can find the real Edgar Allan Poe.

Thank Heaven! the crisis—
The danger is past,
And the lingering illness
Is over at last—
And the fever called "Living"
Is conquered at last.

Sadly, I know
I am shorn of my strength,
And no muscle I move
As I lie at full length—
But no matter!—I feel
I am better at length.

And I rest so composedly
Now, in my bed,
That any beholder
Might fancy me dead—
Might start at beholding me,
Thinking me dead.

The moaning and groaning,
The sighing and sobbing,
Are quieted now,
With that horrible throbbing
At heart:—ah that horrible,
Horrible throbbing!

The sickness—the nausea—
The pitiless pain—
Have ceased, with the fever
That maddened my brain—
With the fever called "Living"
That burned in my brain.

And oh! of all tortures
That torture the worst
Has abated—the terrible
Torture of thirst
For the naphthalene river
Of Passion accurst:—
I have drunk of a water
That quenches all thirst:—

Of a water that flows,
With a lullaby sound,
From a spring but a very few
Feet under ground—
From a cavern not very far
Down under ground.

shorn–*deprived* composedly–*calmly* abated–*stopped* naphthalene–*cleansing* accurst–*cursed*

And ah! let it never
  Be foolishly said
That my room it is gloomy
  And narrow my bed;
For man never slept
  In a different bed—
And, to *sleep*, you must slumber
  In just such a bed.

My tantalized spirit
  Here blandly reposes,
Forgetting, or never
  Regretting, its roses—
Its old agitations
  Of myrtles and roses:

For now, while so quietly
  Lying, it fancies
A holier odor
  About it, of pansies—
A rosemary odor,
  Commingled with pansies—
With rue and the beautiful
  Puritan pansies.

And so it lies happily,
  Bathing in many
A dream of the truth
  And the beauty of Annie—
Drowned in a bath
  Of the tresses of Annie.

She tenderly kissed me,
  She fondly caressed,
And then I fell gently
  To sleep on her breast—
Deeply to sleep
  From the heaven of her breast.

When the light was extinguished,
  She covered me warm,
And she prayed to the angels
  To keep me from harm—
To the queen of the angels
  To shield me from harm.

And I lie so composedly,
  Now, in my bed,
(Knowing her love)
  That you fancy me dead—
And I rest so contentedly,
  Now, in my bed,
(With her love at my breast)
  That you fancy me dead—
That you shudder to look at me,
  Thinking me dead:—

But my heart it is brighter
  Than all of the many
Stars of the sky,
  For it sparkles with Annie—
It glows with the light
  Of the love of my Annie—
With the thought of the light
  Of the eyes of my Annie.

---

tantalized–*tormented*

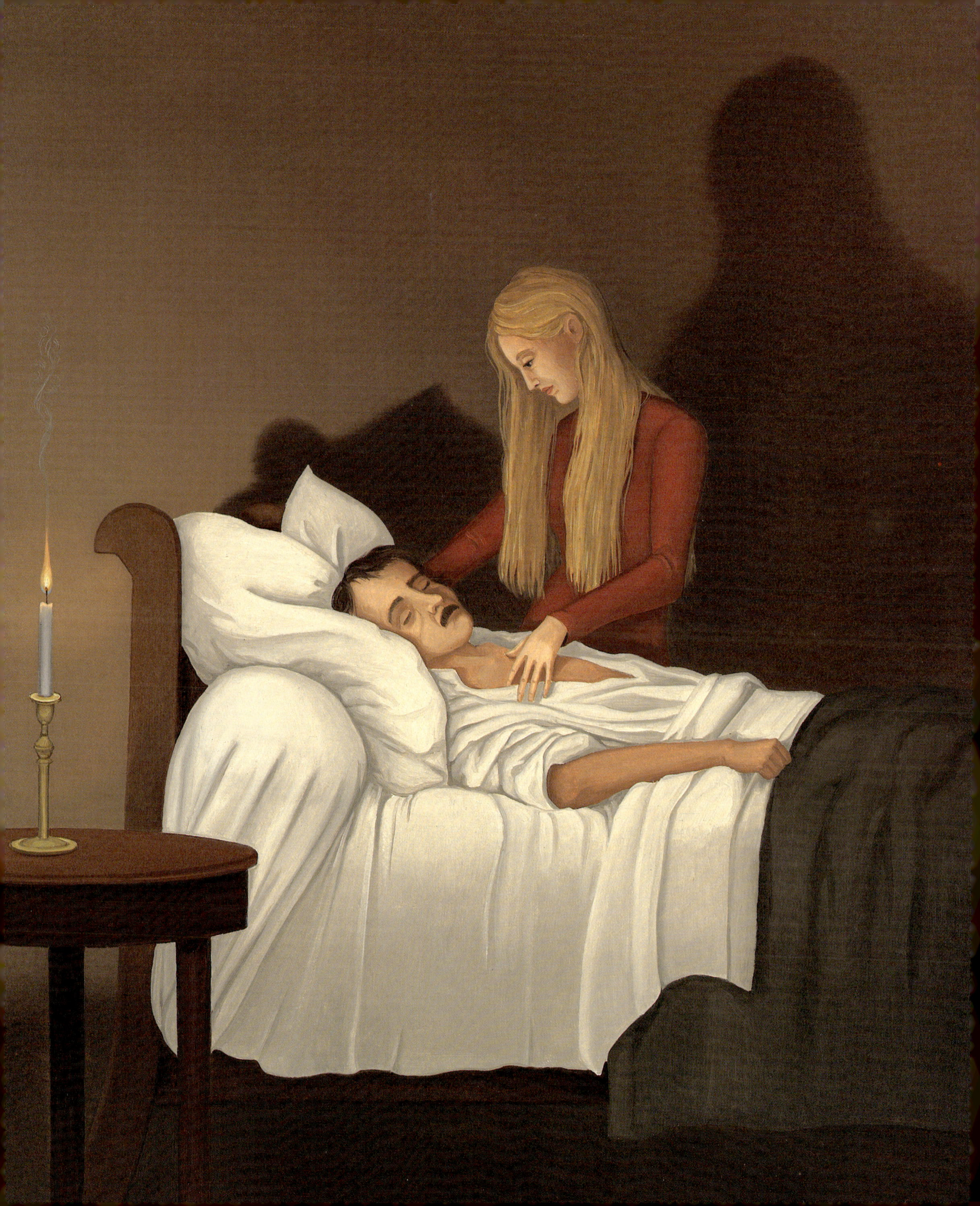

Eulalie—A Song

This poem should encourage young poets. It proves that even a great poet can sometimes write a not-too-great poem. These verses are in the voice of a man very much in love with his wife. In the third to last line, "Astarté" refers to a heavenly body so bright that it shines even during daylight. This is probably the moon. Astarté, the mother goddess of Phoenicia, is often incorrectly believed to be a moon goddess.

I dwelt alone
In a world of moan,
And my soul was a stagnant tide,
Till the fair and gentle Eulalie became my blushing bride—
Till the yellow-haired young Eulalie became my smiling bride.

Ah, less—less bright
The stars of the night
Than the eyes of the radiant girl!
And never a flake
That the vapor can make
With the moon-tints of purple and pearl,
Can vie with the modest Eulalie's most unregarded curl—
Can compare with the bright-eyed Eulalie's most humble and careless curl.

Now Doubt—now Pain
Come never again,
For her soul gives me sigh for sigh,
And all day long
Shines, bright and strong,
Astarté within the sky,
While ever to her dear Eulalie upturns her matron eye—
While ever to her young Eulalie upturns her violet eye.

To _____ _____

Poe addresses this poem to an unnamed woman. He tells her that she is wonderful, so if she wants to be loved, she should simply be herself, and the world will take it as its "duty" to love her. This poem appears in several versions, each dedicated to a different lady. Perhaps Poe used this poem to meet girls. The text was never published, but appears in an undated but clearly authentic manuscript.

Thou wouldst be loved?—then let thy heart
From its present pathway part not!
Being everything which now thou art,
Be nothing which thou are not.
So, with the world, thy winning ways,
Thy truth, thy youth, thy beauty,
Shall be a daily theme of praise,
And love, no more than duty.

From "The Fall of the House of Usher"

The narrator of this story receives a letter from his boyhood friend, Roderick Usher. Roderick complains of a mysterious illness, so the narrator decides to visit him to see if he can help. In this passage we see for the first time the mysterious House of Usher. The house gives us a strange feeling and sets the stage for what is about to be a very strange story.

During the whole of a dull, dark, and soundless day
In the autumn of the year,
When clouds hung low in the heavens,
I had been passing on horseback through dreary country
And found myself,
As shades of evening drew,
Within view of the melancholy House of Usher.
With an utter depression of soul
I looked upon the house...
  The bleak walls,
  The vacant eye-like windows,
  A few white trunks of decayed trees.
There was an iciness, a sinking, a sickening of the heart,
An unredeemed dreariness of thought.
I paused to think
What was it that so unnerved me in the House of Usher?
It was a mystery all insoluble.

---

insoluble–*unable to be solved*

From "The Pit and the Pendulum"

This passage describes the moment at which a man is sentenced to death. Later in the story the man is tortured by a deadly sharp pendulum that swings, like the relentless arm of a giant clock, ever lower above his chest.

The sentence—the dread sentence of death—
Was the last which reached my ears.
I heard no more
Yet, for a while, I saw.
I saw the lips of black-robed judges,
Thin to grotesqueness,
Thin with the intensity of their firmness,
Of immovable resolution,
Of stern contempt of human torture.
I saw the decrees of Fate still issuing from those lips.
I saw them writhe with deadly locution.
I saw them fashion the syllables of my name
And I shuddered.
Then my vision fell upon the seven tall candles upon the table.
At first they seemed white slender angels who would save me,
But then the angel forms became spectres,
With heads of flame,
And I saw that from them there would be no help.
And then the figures of the judges vanished.
All swallowed up in a mad running descent...
Then silence,
And stillness,
And night were the universe.

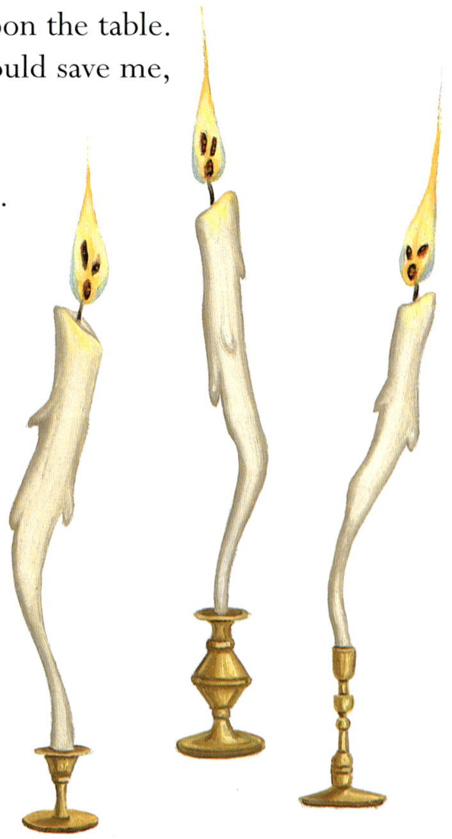

grotesqueness–*deformity* immovable–*unable to be moved* resolution–*determination*
writhe–*to twist in pain* locution–*speech* spectres–*ghosts*

From "The Masque of the Red Death"

This is from a story about a prince who tries to hide from death in a walled castle. He is joined by a thousand of his friends. This passage describes how one night, at a masquerade party, a clock begins to chime. Later in the story, at the stroke of midnight, this same clock will announce the arrival of a strange and deadly visitor.

There stood against the western wall
A gigantic clock of ebony.
Its pendulum swung to and fro
With a dull, heavy, monotonous clang,
And when the minute-hand made the circuit of the face
And the hour was to be stricken,
There came from the brazen lungs of the clock
A sound which was clear and loud and deep
And exceedingly musical,
But of so peculiar a note
That the musicians of the orchestra were constrained to pause
And the waltzers ceased their evolutions,
And there was a brief disconcert of the whole gay company,
And the giddiest grew pale.
But when the echoes had fully ceased,
A light laughter at once pervaded the assembly,
The musicians looked at each other and smiled
And made whispering vows
That the next chiming of the clock should produce no similar emotion;
And then,
After the lapse of sixty minutes,
There came yet another chiming of the clock,
And the same disconcert and meditation as before.

constrained–*forced* evolutions–*twirling movements* disconcert–*worried disturbance*

From "The Tell-Tale Heart"

"The Tell-Tale Heart" is a story about an insane murderer. This passage describes how he prepares to commit his ghastly crime.

You fancy me mad.
Madmen know nothing.
But you should have seen *me.*
You should have seen how wisely I proceeded,
With what caution,
With what foresight.
Every night, about midnight,
I turned the latch of his door
And opened it—oh, so gently!
And then,
When I had made an opening sufficient for my head,
I put in a dark lantern,
All closed so that no light shone out,
And then I thrust in my head.
How cunningly I thrust it in!
I moved it slowly—very, very slowly,
So that I might not disturb the old man's sleep.
It took me an hour.
Ha! Would a mad man have been so wise as this?
And then
I undid it just so much that a single thin ray fell upon the vulture eye.
This I did for seven long nights,
Every night just at midnight,
But I found the eye always closed;
And so it was impossible to do the work
For it was not the old man who vexed me,
But his evil eye.

From "The Black Cat"

In this story, a condemned criminal tells how the howl of a black cat led police to discover the body of his victim.

I rapped heavily, with a cane
Upon that very portion of the brick-work,
But...
No sooner had the reverberation of my blows sunk into silence
I was answered by a voice from within the tomb,
By a cry,
At first muffled and broken, like the sobbing of a child,
And then quickly swelling into one long, loud, and continuous scream,
Utterly inhuman...
A howl...
A wailing shriek...
Half of horror and half of triumph
Such as might have arisen out of hell
From the throats of the damned in their agony
And the demons that exult in the damnation.

reverberation–*echo* exult–*triumph*

From "The Cask of Amontillado"

With the promise of Amontillado wine, the villain of this story leads his victim to a dead end deep in the underground passages of his family tomb. What happens next is perhaps one of the most haunting crimes in the body of English literature.

We continued in search of the Amontillado.
We passed through low arches
And descending again,
Arrived at a deep crypt
In which the foulness of the air
Caused our flambeaux rather to glow than flame.
At the most remote end of the crypt
There appeared another...less spacious.
Its walls had been lined with human bones
Piled to the vault overhead in the fashion of the catacombs.
Within the wall we perceived a still interior recess,
In depth about four feet,
In width three,
In height six or seven.
It seemed to have been constructed for no especial use,
The interval between two colossal supports of the roof,
And backed by one circumscribing wall of solid granite.
He stepped unsteadily forward,
While I followed immediately at his heels.
In an instant he had reached the extremity of the niche,
And finding his progress arrested by the rock,
Stood stupidly bewildered.
A moment more and I had fettered him to the granite.
"The Amontillado!" ejaculated my friend.

---

crypt–*underground passage* flambeaux–*torches* catacombs–*underground cemetery with spaces for corpses* colossal–*giant* circumscribing–*enclosing* niche–*hollow place in a wall* fettered–*bound with chains* ejaculated–*spoke out suddenly*

From "HOP-FROG"

This story is about a king who has a court jester, a dwarf named Hop-Frog. The king forces the jester to drink wine, even though he knows it will make him crazy and sick. In the end the jester destroys the king. When we read this story, it's easy to believe that Poe knew his alcohol addiction was bad for him and that he wished, like little Hop-Frog, that he could get rid of it.

"Come here, Hop-Frog," said the king,
"Swallow this
And then let us have the benefit of your invention.
We want characters—
Characters, man, something novel.
We are wearied with this everlasting sameness.
Come drink!
The wine will brighten your wits."
The command to drink forced the tears to Hop-Frog's eyes,
Bitter drops fell into the goblet as he took it,
Humbly,
From the hand of the tyrant.
"Ha! Ha! Ha!" roared the king,
As the dwarf reluctantly drained the beaker.
Poor fellow!
Hop-Frog's large eyes gleamed…
He placed the goblet nervously on the table,
And looked round upon the company with a half-insane stare.

From "THE PREMATURE BURIAL"

This is a bright spot from an otherwise very dark story about a man who lives with a fear of being buried alive. Unlike most of Poe's characters, he avoids the unhappy ending.

Out of evil proceeded good—
  My soul acquired tone,
  I went abroad,
  I took vigorous exercise,
  I breathed the free air of Heaven,
  I thought upon other subjects than Death,
  And I read no bugaboo tales—such as this.
In short I became a new man,
And lived life.

bugaboo–*ghost*

Index